ZIPPY LEARNS...
EVERYONE IS IMPORTANT!

WRITTEN BY: MARY-ELLEN KRAMER   ILLUSTRATED BY: JIM MAYFIELD

Printed and bound in Canada by Art Bookbindery

www.ArtBookbindery.com

ISBN 978-0-615-42826-0

It was another fun Saturday morning at the ice rink! The children were very excited to skate. They were lacing up their skates and putting on their helmets. Everyone's favorite ice-resurfacing machine, Zippy, was starting his workday. Zippy's job was to smooth out the ice so that everyone can skate. This was Zippy's important job, and he loved it.

Whenever Zippy came out onto the rink, children always cheered and waved. They enjoyed watching him smooth the ice. "I love my job," thought Zippy as he drove out. But today was a very busy day at the ice rink. A lot was happening. There were ice-skating lessons, hockey-team practices, and free-time skating. The rink was full, and everyone was busy making sure they were following the schedule.

As Zippy smoothed out the ice, he smiled at the children and waited for their cheers. But the children were so busy today that they forgot to cheer. Busy, busy, busy. "Hello, boys and girls!" shouted Zippy. But nobody heard him. Zippy felt sad that the children forgot to cheer for him. He didn't understand. "Why isn't anyone happy to see me?" he wondered.

Next, Zippy decided to say hello to Mr. Frank, the owner of the ice rink. Mr. Frank was always happy to see Zippy. "Hello, Mr. Frank!" cried Zippy. But Mr. Frank was too busy talking on the telephone, and he did not hear Zippy. "What is happening?" Zippy asked himself. Zippy wondered why nobody had the time to talk to him today. "I feel invisible," he said at the end of the day. "I'm not important."

Later that night, Zippy could not fall asleep. "I wish I knew what to do," he said. Suddenly, Zippy thought of something. "I have an idea!" he exclaimed. "I will run away from the ice rink. I am not needed here. I will find a new job where I am important." So Zippy left the ice rink and headed down the long road.

He drove for a long time, and then he saw a truck. "Hello, friend!" said the truck "My name is Dan, and I'm a dump truck." "Hello, Dan," said Zippy. "My name is Zippy, and I'm an ice-resurfacing machine. I am running away from the ice rink. I want to find a job where I'm important." "Would you like to work with me?" asked Dan. "Sure!" answered Zippy, and off they went to Dan's job.

"I carry dirt from one place to another," explained Dan. "That is my job." "Oh, I think I can do that too!" said Zippy. Dan dumped his dirt onto the ground. "Your turn," said Dan. But Zippy didn't have any dirt to dump. He did not have a place to keep dirt. "This isn't going to work," said Zippy. So he went back on the road again to find a new job.

Next, Zippy saw a bus. "Hello, friend!" said the bus. "My name is Sally, and I'm a school bus." "Hello, Sally," said Zippy. "My name is Zippy, and I'm an ice-resurfacing machine. I am running away from the ice rink. I want to find a job where I'm important," he explained. "Would you like to work with me?" asked Sally. "Sure!" answered Zippy, and off they went to Sally's job.

"I take children to school," said Sally. That is my job."
"Oh, I think I can do that too!" said Zippy. Zippy watched
the children board Sally. "Your turn," said Sally. But
Zippy didn't have any seats. "This isn't going to work,"
said Zippy. So he went back on the road again to find
a new job.

Next, Zippy saw a red truck. "Hello, friend!" said the red truck. "My name is Freddie, and I'm a fire truck." "Hello, Freddie," said Zippy. "My name is Zippy, and I'm an ice-resurfacing machine. I am running away from the ice rink. I want to find a job where I'm important." "Would you like to work with me?" asked Freddie. "Sure!" answered Zippy, and off they went to Freddie's job.

"I put out fires," said Freddie. "That is my job." "Oh, I think I can do that too!" said Zippy. Zippy watched Freddie put out a fire. "Your turn," said Freddie. But Zippy didn't have any hoses. "This isn't going to work," said Zippy. So he went back on the road again to find a new job.

Suddenly, Zippy saw cars driving by him, and they looked very upset. He stopped one of them and asked, "What's wrong?" "Something happened at the ice rink today," answered one of the cars. "Nobody could skate on the ice. We are taking all of the children home." Zippy decided to go back to the ice rink. He wondered why nobody could skate.

What was the problem? Zippy decided to ask Mr. Frank. "He will tell me what happened here," thought Zippy. He found Mr. Frank sitting in the bleachers looking worried. "Mr. Frank?" asked Zippy, "What is wrong?"

"Oh, Zippy!" Mr. Frank exclaimed. "You weren't here. There was nobody here to do your job. The ice got too bumpy, and the children couldn't skate. I had to send everyone home. Where were you, Zippy?"

"I didn't think I was important here anymore. Yesterday the children forgot to cheer for me," explained Zippy. "I ran away. I tried to be a dump truck, but I couldn't carry dirt," said Zippy. "I tried to be a school bus, but I didn't have any seats for the children. I tried to be a fire truck, but I didn't have any hoses."

"But, Zippy," Mr. Frank explained, "You are an ice-resurfacing machine. Nobody else can do your job. You are very important. The children can't skate without you." "I'm important?" asked Zippy. "Yes," answered Mr. Frank. "Yesterday everyone was too busy to cheer for you. But you are still important, and you are always needed here." Zippy started to understand. "Even if people forget to cheer for me, I am still needed very much here. I'm the only one who can do my job."

The next day, Zippy came out to smooth the ice, and the children cheered for him. "Thank you, Zippy," they cheered. "Yesterday we couldn't skate without you! You are so important to us." Zippy was so happy to be back at the ice rink. "I am important!" he said.

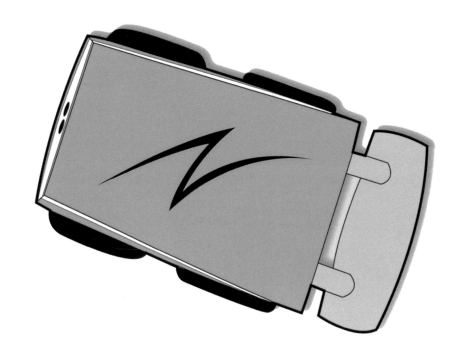

THE END

Did you find the hidden Z on each page?